There's a Monster Eating My House

by Art Cumings

PARENTS MAGAZINE PRESS / NEW YORK

Library of Congress Cataloging in Publication Data
Cumings, Art.   There's a monster eating my house.
SUMMARY: Sir William helps a house-eating monster
change its diet.
[1. Monsters—Fiction]   I. Title.
PZ7.C9097Th   [E]   80-25378
ISBN 0-8193-1053-0
ISBN 0-8193-1054-9 (lib. bdg.)

to Alda

Sir William was in his castle
one morning with his friends
Clarence, Harvey, and Hattie.

Suddenly his phone rang.
"Hello," Sir William said.
"May I help you?"
"Come quick!" said Burly.
"There's a monster eating my house!"

"What does it look like?"
Sir William asked.
"It's the ugliest monster
I've ever seen," said Burly.
"It's half animal and half machine."

CRUNCH

CRUNCH

CRUNCH

"Does it puff black smoke
and have an awful smell?"
Sir William asked.
"Yes!" said Burly.

"It's the Machinosaurus!"
Sir William said.
"I'll be there before
you can count to three."

Burly started to count.
"One, two, ..."
But before he could say "three,"
Burly's doorbell rang.
It was Sir William.

Burly opened his door
only wide enough
to poke his paw through
and point to the back of his house.

Sir William looked behind Burly's house.
All he found was a large hole,
some half-eaten stones,
and part of a porch door.
Burly's back porch was gone . . .

and so was the Machinosaurus.

Sir William felt bad.
It was his job to catch monsters,
and he had failed.
But he had no idea where
to look for the Machinosaurus.

Sir William returned to his castle.
He had hung up his armor and
just turned on the TV when . . .

Brrring! The phone rang.
It was Ollie.
"Come quick!" he said.
"There's a monster eating my house!"

"What does it look like?"
Sir William asked.
"It's half animal and half machine,"
said Ollie.

"It puffs black smoke and
has an awful smell."
"It's the Machinosaurus!" Sir William said.
"I'll be there before
you can count to three."

Ollie began to count.
But before he reached three,
he heard Sir William shouting,
"Where is that monster?"
There was a big hole
in the side of Ollie's cellar.
There were giant teeth marks
all over it.
But there was no Machinosaurus.

"Sorry," Sir William said.
"If only I had an idea
where to look for it."
Ollie pointed to a path
of broken trees.

"How about looking there?" he said.
Sir William and his friends
followed the path
for only a few minutes.
Then they stopped.

"This path is leading straight
towards Mrs. Water's house,"
Sir William said.
"Do you think this Machinosaurus
is mean enough to harm
Mrs. Water's house?"

"No monster is that mean,"
said Hattie.
"Mrs. Water is so kind
and makes such delicious pies."

Sir William was glad
when he arrived at Mrs. Water's house.
It was not harmed and
there was no monster in sight.

Sir William took off his helmet.
He was about to treat his friends
to one of Mrs. Water's
delicious pies when . . .

"EEEOOW!" cried Clarence.
Towering above Mrs. Water's trees
was the Machinosaurus.
It was eating the top of a tree
and puffing black smoke.
"How can anyone be so mean?"
said Harvey.
"I say we teach it some manners!"

"Hold it!" Sir William said.
"This Machinosaurus is acting very strange,
and I would like to know why.
Why did it eat only a porch?
It could have eaten the whole house.

Why did it eat only a cellar
and why is it eating only
the top of that tree?
There is only one way to find out.
I must ask the monster."

And so he did.

"Pardon me," said Sir William,
"but why are you eating only
the top of that tree?"
"Trees taste awful," said the monster.
"Then why eat them?" Sir William said.
"Because houses taste just as bad,
and I have to eat something."
"Hmm," Sir William thought.
Then he asked the monster,
"Have you ever eaten a pie?"

"A pie? What is a pie?"
asked the Machinosaurus.
"Taste one," Sir William said.

"Wow!" The monster smiled.
"I have never tasted anything this good!"

Sir William whispered to Mrs. Water.
She went into her house and came out
with a whole stack of pies.

"Here!" Sir William said.

"But you must promise
never to eat another
porch, tree, or cellar. Promise?"
"I promise!" said the Machinosaurus.

Sir William was pleased.
He could tell by the monster's smile
and the way it licked
its giant jaws that
it would keep its promise.

He said good-bye to Mrs. Water
and to the Machinosaurus
and then he returned to his castle.

He had just hung up his armor
and sat down
when there was a knock
at the door.
It was Mrs. Water's delivery man.
He had the biggest pie
Sir William had ever seen.
And on it, printed in whipped cream,
were two words ...

ABOUT THE AUTHOR/ARTIST

When Art Cumings sits down to illustrate
a story, he thinks carefully about the
characters and he imagines the place they
live. He puts in so many details that it looks
as if he has visited the place in real life.
"The most important thing to do," he says,
"is to create a whole world that someone can
believe in, and that's fun."

Mr. Cumings created the visual world for
stories written by many other authors before
going on to write and illustrate his own
book, THERE'S A MONSTER EATING MY
HOUSE. Of these, four titles were for
Parents, including MAGIC GROWING
POWDER by Janet Quin-Harkin. His
illustrations have also appeared in many
magazines.

Mr. Cumings lives with his wife in
Douglaston, N.Y.